This Summer
Rest, Relax and
Read!

Sign up for
Summer Reading at
Kirkwoodpubliclibrary.org

Aunt Minnie and the Twister

by Mary Skillings Prigger

Illustrated by Betsy Lewin

CLARION BOOKS • NEW YORK

**To Tori, Kurt, Riley, Holly, Madelynn, and Emily,
who are always sources of inspiration
—M.S.P.**

**To Floyd and Stella Dickman
—B. L.**

Clarion Books
a Houghton Mifflin Company imprint
215 Park Avenue South, New York, NY 10003
Text copyright © 2002 by Mary Skillings Prigger
Illustrations copyright © 2002 by Betsy Lewin

The illustrations were executed in watercolor.
The text was set in 15-point New Century Schoolbook.

www.houghtonmifflinbooks.com

Printed in Singapore

Library of Congress Cataloging-in-Publication Data

Prigger, Mary Skillings.
Aunt Minnie and the twister / Mary Skillings Prigger ; illustrations by Betsy Lewin.
    p.   cm.
Summary: After a tornado rearranges their Kansas house, Aunt Minnie and the nine nieces
and nephews living with her add on a much-needed new room.
ISBN 0-618-11136-0
[1. Tornadoes—Fiction. 2. Farm life—Kansas—Fiction. 3. Aunts—Fiction. 4. Kansas—Fiction.]
I. Lewin, Betsy, ill. II. Title.   PZ7.P93534 As 2002   [E]—dc21   2001037249

TWP 10 9 8 7 6 5 4 3 2 1

Minnie McGranahan lived in a little house
on a little farm in Kansas.

She had nine orphaned nieces and nephews,
and they all lived with her.
They called her "Aunt Minnie."

As Aunt Minnie's kids grew, the little house became
more and more crowded.
Sometimes the kids were cross, and sometimes they complained.
Minnie said, "Well, we don't have much room—
but we have each other."

When Minnie wanted her kids' attention,
she stood on the front porch and rang an old school bell.
CLANG, CLANG, CLANG went the bell.
Aunt Minnie's kids came running.

The bell called them for supper. It said, "Don't be late."

It summoned them when there was trouble.
"Come quick, the cows are out!" Aunt Minnie shouted.

The bell rang when there was company.
"Wash up. Preacher Bill is here to call. Let's look like proper folks," Aunt Minnie said.

Come spring, Minnie and her kids planted and hoed the garden.
They made a scarecrow and put Aunt Minnie's old dress and hat
on it to frighten the birds away.
"Can't have those birds harvesting our crops before we do,"
laughed Minnie.

In the summer, they picked corn, beans, tomatoes,
and peas and canned them for the winter.
"This will be good eating when it's cold outside,"
Aunt Minnie told her kids.

In the fall, when the leaves began to turn,
Minnie and her kids picked apples.
She showed the children how to make apple butter, applesauce,
and apple cider.

They put turnips, potatoes, and carrots in barrels and stored them
in the root cellar in the hill beside the house.

The younger kids resisted going into the root cellar.
Little snakes and toads liked to hide in the cool places.
The snakes slithered into cracks and corners.
Toads jumped out when a hand reached inside a barrel.

But Aunt Minnie wasn't afraid. She would scoop up
the critters in her apron and shake them outside.

When winter came and snow covered the ground,
Minnie and the kids gathered the food they had stored
in the root cellar.
"Yum," they said when they spread apple butter on their bread.
"It tastes just like summertime."

One spring day, storm clouds rolled across the sky. Aunt Minnie told her kids, "We need to do our chores, but listen for the bell. If it looks like it's fixin' to storm bad, I'll ring the bell. You come running home."

The clouds got blacker and blacker. Lightning flashed.
Minnie rushed to the front porch and rang the bell.
CLANG, CLANG, CLANG. "Come quick!" it said.
Minnie's kids came running from the hen house,
from the barn, and from the garden.

Minnie pointed at the sky, where a large funnel-shaped cloud was forming.
"Twister!" she shouted. "Hold on to each other and run for the root cellar!"

The oldest kids grabbed the youngest.
The ones in the middle grabbed each other.
They all held on to Aunt Minnie as they pushed
against the wind.

They tugged and pulled the cellar doors open,
and fell in a heap on the root cellar floor.
BANG! Aunt Minnie slammed the doors behind them.

SMACK! CRACK! went the hailstones against the doors.
WHOOOSH roared the wind.
The doors strained and groaned.
Aunt Minnie and her kids huddled together in the dark.
They were safe inside the root cellar.

No one said a word about snakes or toads.

Suddenly it was quiet.

"Shhh," said Aunt Minnie. "Listen!"

Croak, croak. Croak, croak.

"It's the toads!" said one of the boys.

"They're telling us the storm is over."

"We made it!" the children cheered.

"And we still have each other!" said Aunt Minnie.

"Now, let's see what mischief the twister did."

They pushed open the cellar doors and spilled outside.
They couldn't believe what they saw.
"LAND SAKES!" exclaimed Aunt Minnie.
"LAND SAKES!" exclaimed the kids.

"I don't believe it," Aunt Minnie sighed.
The twister had cut a path through the fields.
Aunt Minnie's Model T Ford was on its side.
The hen house and the scarecrow were gone.
The chickens were scattered all over the farm.
The cows were in the front yard.

Most amazing of all was Aunt Minnie's house.
It was still standing.
But it had been turned around!
The front was facing the johnny house,
and the back was in the front!

Aunt Minnie didn't say a word.
She took the two littlest children by the hand
and led her kids in a parade around the house.

First they walked one way. Then the other.
They checked up and down and all around.

Finally Aunt Minnie announced, "Well, this will never do!
We can't have a topsy-turvy house.
We can't have the front door facing the johnny house.

33

"And we can't very well turn the house back around.
So we will just have to make a new front.
We can build another room onto the new back.
Our family is getting too big for this little house anyway."
"Hurrah!" shouted the children.

So they sold two calves, a brood of chicks, and the next crop of corn
to buy building supplies.
Minnie hired a carpenter from town.
He worked and worked, and Aunt Minnie and all the kids pitched in.
They all worked together to build the new room.

35

When the work was done, they had a picnic to celebrate the new room on the back of the old front of the little house. And Aunt Minnie's kids knew they had a home for as long as they wanted.

And, most important, they had each other.